CLYDE the HiPPO
CLYDE LIED

by Keith Marantz

illustrated by Larissa Marantz

PENGUIN WORKSHOP

W

PENGUIN WORKSHOP
An Imprint of Penguin Random House LLC, New York

Text copyright © 2020 by Keith Marantz. Illustrations copyright © 2020 by Larissa Marantz. All rights reserved. Published by Penguin Workshop, an imprint of Penguin Random House LLC, New York. PENGUIN and PENGUIN WORKSHOP are trademarks of Penguin Books Ltd, and the W colophon is a registered trademark of Penguin Random House LLC. Manufactured in China.

Visit us online at www.penguinrandomhouse.com.

Library of Congress Cataloging-in-Publication Data is available upon request.

ISBN 9780593094518 (pbk)   10 9 8 7 6 5 4 3 2 1
ISBN 9780593094525 (hc)   10 9 8 7 6 5 4 3 2 1

For Alek, Kela, and Sasha
—KM & LM

This is Clyde.

He's headed back to school after a long break.
He can't wait to see his friends again!

"Hi, Amanda!" Clyde exclaims. "How was your vacation?"

"It was fun!" says Amanda. "I went skiing down a really steep mountain at lightning speed!"

"That's nothing," says Toby. "I surfed a twenty-foot wave. I got a sunburn, but it was totally worth it."

"Well, top this!" Dot says. "I went camping and caught *buckets* of fish."

"Wow," Clyde says with a sigh. "That all sounds amazing."

"Where did you go?" asks Toby.

Everyone stares at Clyde.

"Ummm, well, I went to . . . SPACE CAMP!"
Clyde says.

Everyone gasps. "Ooohhhhhh!"

"Yeah . . . we got to take a trip to OUTER SPACE!"
Clyde continues. "And we landed on Mars, and
met a real live Martian and took a picture with him!
His name was Phillip!"

"Really?" Toby asks. "I don't believe you.
I want to see that picture of Phillip."

"Yeah!" say Dot and Amanda.

"Uh—I'll bring it tomorrow," Clyde mumbles.

Clyde knows he has gone too far.

At home, he wonders where he's going to get a photo of himself with an alien.

Maybe Orson can help, he thinks.

First, Clyde tries to paint Orson
green, like a Martian.

But Clyde starts to look like a Martian, too.

Then Clyde decides that Orson needs another eye.

But it keeps falling off.

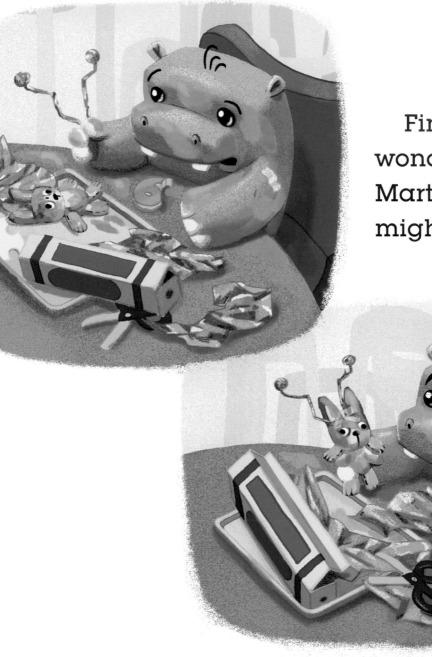

Finally, Clyde
wonders if some
Martian antennae
might do the trick.

But while aluminum foil is great for wrapping peanut butter and banana sandwiches, it is not so good for making Martian antennae.

Clyde is not having much luck turning Orson into an alien. In fact, Orson is now a mess! Clyde notices all the trash on the ground. Was all the trouble he went through to hide the truth really worth it?

Clyde knows he is going to have to face his friends and tell them he lied.

The next day at school, Clyde's friends gather around him.

"Well, where is it?" Toby asks. "Let's see that alien photo!"

"I have something to tell you," Clyde says. "I lied. I made up that story so you wouldn't make fun of me for not going on a cool trip like you all did."

"Clyde, I have something to tell you, too," says Amanda. "I didn't really go down a steep ski slope. I stayed where it was flat, and I barely moved at all."

"I didn't really catch buckets of fish," Dot adds. "I only caught one. And it got away because it slipped out of my paws!"

"I lied, too," Toby says. "I'm actually scared of the ocean. But I *did* get sunburned."

"Well, I did watch a *Three Green Friends* movie at home," says Clyde. "And it was great!"

"I LOVE *Three Green Friends*!" says Amanda.

"Me too!" adds Dot.

"Maybe my family will go somewhere for the next school break," Clyde says. "But if we don't, that's fine with me."

"Maybe next time, we can all come over and watch *Three Green Friends* together!" says Toby.

"That would be out of this world!" Clyde exclaims.

And it was.